Sleep, Little One, Sleep

BY Marion Dane Bauer

ILLUSTRATED BY JoEllen McAllister Stammen

Simon & Schuster Books for Young Readers

SIMON & SCHUSTER BOOKS FOR YOUNG READERS
An imprint of Simon & Schuster Children's Publishing Division
1230 Avenue of the Americas, New York, New York 10020
Text copyright © 1999 by Marion Dane Bauer
Illustrations copyright © 1999 by JoEllen McAllister Stammen
All rights reserved including the right of reproduction in whole or in part in any form.
SIMON & SCHUSTER BOOKS FOR YOUNG READERS is a trademark of Simon & Schuster.
Book design by Paul Zakris. The text for this book is set in 26-point Weiss.
Printed in Hong Kong
10 9 8 7 6 5 4 3 2 1

LIBRARY OF CONGRESS CATALOGING-IN-PUBLICATION DATA
Bauer, Marion Dane.
Sleep, Little One, Sleep / by Marion Dane Bauer ;
illustrated by JoEllen McAllister Stammen. — 1st ed.
p.   cm.
Summary: Sleepiness is compared to the actions of
a spider, a mouse, a bird, and increasingly larger animals.
ISBN 0-689-82250-2
[1.Animals—Infancy—Fiction. 2. Bedtime—
Fiction.] I. McAllister Stammen, JoEllen, ill. II. Title.
PZ7.B3262Sl 1999
[E]—dc21   98-19567   CIP   AC

A NOTE FROM THE ARTIST
The artwork for this book was done in dry pastel on dark gray pastel paper.
The original art is much larger than the size of the printed pieces in order to
strengthen the details and the colors in the illustrations.

For Maho, from your
American grandma, with love
—M. D. B.

To the One who gives sweet sleep and true rest
—J. M. S.

Come, little one. The day is done.
Sleep spins a web, delicate and strong,
To cradle you.
To cradle you.

Even the weary sun shuts its glowing eye.

Sleep nibbles the last crumbs of day.

Don't scare it off!

Don't scare it off!

Now, now, beloved. Snuggle close.

Sleep gathers you beneath its feathery wings.

Safe and warm.

Safe and warm.

I'll tuck you in. Sweetheart, lie still.

Sleep nuzzles your cheek, licks your pearly ear.

Feel its warm breath.

Feel its warm breath.

Be patient. Sleep will come,
trudging closer, closer, careful and slow.
Just you wait!
Just you wait!

Sleep is woolly. Sleep is warm.
It grazes softly around your bed.
Cuddle close.
Cuddle close.

Look! See it there?

Sleep creeps in on velvet paws.

Hear it purr?

Hear it purr?

Be ready, child. Sleep is near.

It stamps, stamps, stirs the dust.

Rub your eyes!

Rub your eyes!

Now's the time. Close your eyes.

Sleep holds you tight in the furry dark.

Hugs you close.

Hugs you close.

Hush, my darling. Hush, my dear.

Plunge down, down into the dark.

Deep and deep.

Sleep and sleep.

Sleep watches in the night. Sleep smiles from above.

Sleep shines from here to tomorrow.

Lighting your way to dreams.

Lighting your way to dreams.

Do you see, my angel? There and there?

Sleep winks and blinks in a darkening sky.

Let it come.

Please . . . let it come!

Sleep, little one, . . .

. . . sleep.